INTERPLANETARY Weather Bulletin

Dear Reader

Most of us are interested in learning what the weather will be like tomorrow. Will it be raining or windy or sunny?

I was watching a weather bulletin on TV when I thought, "I wonder what the weather forecasts will be like in a hundred years?"

> "WE'LL BE CROSSING LIVE TO OUR REPORTERS THROUGHOUT THE SOLAR SYSTEM FOR UPDATES ON WHAT SORT OF A DAY IT'S BEEN IN OUR LITTLE SPOT WITHIN THE ORION ARM OF THE MILKY WAY GALAXY."

If climate change keeps occurring, no doubt the weather in most places on Earth would be very different. But then I also thought that, by that time, we might be reporting the weather from all over the solar system. An interplanetary weather bulletin might go something like this ...

John Parsons

Contents

INTERPLANETARY Weather Bu

1 Welcome to the Interplanetary Weather Bulletin!

Live Throughout the **Solar System**

Good evening viewers, and welcome to tonight's edition of the Interplanetary Weather Bulletin. I'm Poppy Mono-Squint, and tonight we're broadcasting from the Orbital Broadcasting Corporation's studio just beyond the asteroid belt between Mars and Jupiter. We'll be crossing live to our reporters throughout the solar system for updates on what sort of a day it's been in our little spot within the Orion arm of the Milky Way galaxy. We'll also be taking a look at what the weather's going to look like at your place over the next few days.

First up, let's take a look at today's highs and lows throughout the region. No surprises in the major centres, with Mercury hitting a frosty overnight low of –183 °C and an afternoon high of 427 °C.

Venusians have been enjoying a fairly constant 480 °C during their day and night, so let's hope the air conditioning is working or there'll be plenty of tossing and turning for our friends on Venus. Earth's average temperature came in at a pleasant 15 °C, which is a long way from its record high of 57.8 °C and its record low of –89 °C. It's been a lovely day on Mars, with the high at the equator climbing to 20 °C, but wrap up warm, because those temperatures will be dropping to a bracing –90 °C tonight. Those of you swirling around in the upper layers of Jupiter's gas clouds experienced a balmy 21 °C throughout the day, while further out, there was a nippy day on Saturn's surface, with temperatures steady at –138 °C.

If you didn't pack the right clothes for a long summer on Uranus, you'll be feeling those –184 °C days right now, but at –218 °C, the folks on Neptune will be wondering what you're worried about. Meanwhile, beyond the planets, in the remotest provinces, Pluto is experiencing record highs as it comes closer to the Sun than it's been for centuries, with a whopping –235 °C recorded at around lunchtime today.

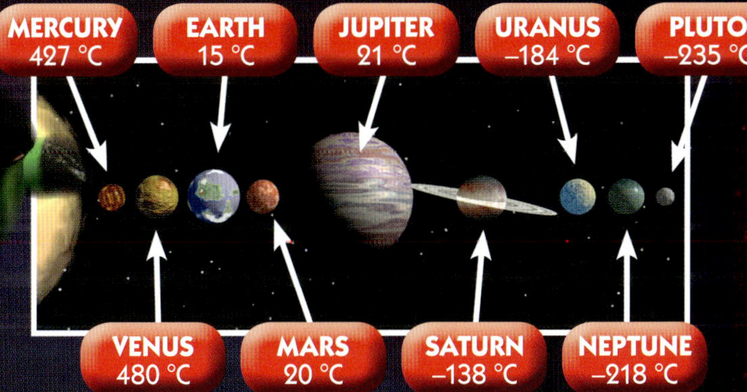

Well, there are today's highs and lows, now let's see what tomorrow has in store for you. No matter where you are in the solar system, whether the Sun's just another twinkling star or a huge fiery orb in your skies, whether you've been sweltering or shivering, this yellow dwarf is the star that keeps us all together. Let's begin tomorrow's forecast with a look at what's brewing in the centre of our solar system.

Following some unsettled solar weather patterns, a burst of solar wind was ejected from the Sun yesterday, reaching speeds of up to 500 kilometres per second. When the associated magnetic fields and charged particles hit Earth's atmosphere, there were reports of a colourful aurora in areas around the North Pole. Due to its lack of a magnetic field, exposed areas of Mars can expect to lose some of their scarce atmosphere when the solar wind hits in a couple of days, but, on the bright side, it'll be a good day for getting that washing dry.

Reports from the solar monitoring satellite indicate that solar activity is expected to be low with a chance of some minor disturbances. Surface temperatures on the Sun are expected to be around 5 500 °C, but there's a couple of cooler sunspots holding the mercury down to 4 200 °C in their vicinity, and they're being tracked just in case they join up and cause a solar flare. The geomagnetic field around the Sun is expected to be unsettled to active, with isolated minor storm periods possible and a slight chance for a small proton burst – so if you're travelling between planets tomorrow, make sure you keep your radiation suits handy.

It's time for a break, but don't go away, because right after these commercials, we'll be taking a look at what's in store for Mercury tomorrow.

THE SUN

The Sun is the star at the centre of the solar system. All eight planets (and Pluto, a dwarf planet) move around the Sun in elliptical orbits.

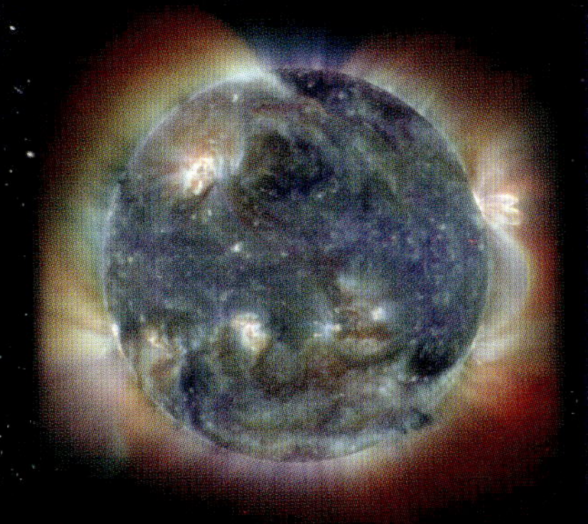

This image of the Sun (above) has been taken by cameras that don't capture light, but capture magnetic fields and radiation bursts that are invisible to the human eye. It shows bursts of highly radioactive particles being ejected from the Sun in vast clouds and waves. These travel out into space, and are known as "solar wind".

Astronomers classify stars by size and apparent temperature. The hottest stars are blue. Temperatures then cool through white, yellow, orange and red, down to brown, which is the coolest.

The largest stars are called supergiants. Medium-sized stars are known as giants. Small stars are known as dwarfs.

The Sun is a yellow dwarf, which means it is a small star of medium heat. By comparison, blue supergiants may generate more than a million times the Sun's heat!

SUN FACTS

The Sun, which is made up mostly of hydrogen and helium gas, makes up 99.8% of the weight of the entire solar system. All the other planets combined form the other 0.2%. The Sun is like a massive thermonuclear reactor where, in its centre, 620 million tonnes of hydrogen are converted into helium each second!

2 Mercury

Tempting Temperatures

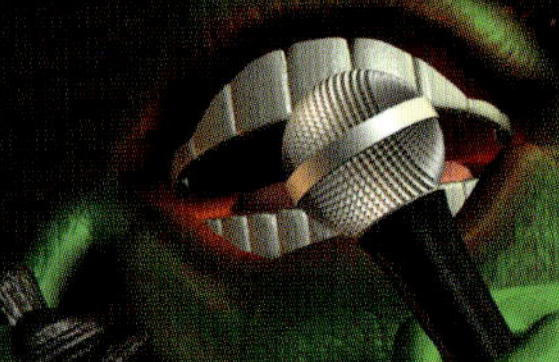

Welcome back, everybody. Now, let's cross live to our weather reporter on the surface of Mercury, Bob Harrison. I'm guessing you'll be looking for some nice shady spots there, Bob?

INTERPLANETARY WEATHER BULLETIN

MERCURY LIVE!

Thanks, Poppy, and you're right, with another day of temperature swings of up to 610 °C predicted, we won't be venturing too far from home tomorrow! Due to the lack of atmosphere here, there's just no insulation, so when the Sun's beating down on us, it's hot. But there's nothing to hold that heat in. Even though we're the closest planet to that familiar yellow dwarf, when the Sun's not overhead, temperatures on Mercury can drop low enough for the folks at least 2.8 billion kilometres away on Uranus to be comfortable with.

Another consequence of the lack of atmosphere means there's no air or dust to split the Sun's light into different colours, so we won't be seeing any blue skies tomorrow. It'll just be black skies as always, with a huge Sun hovering overhead.

Actually, when I say tomorrow, I'm just kidding, of course. Mercury rotates so slowly that our "days" are 59 Earth days long. What's even more bizarre is that we orbit the Sun at a faster speed than we rotate. That means that the Sun is actually visible in the sky for 176 days – but after a Mercury noon, it appears to travel backwards for a while.

In terms of the weather forecast on Mercury, it's pretty much more of the same. No atmosphere means no weather, just some wild temperature fluctuations. The only warning we have is for drivers to watch out for ice from comets that have landed on the shady side of craters at the poles. Yes, even on Mercury, there are a few frosty areas. Unlike all the other planets, we don't tilt over on our axis, so there are no seasons and the Sun's always low in the sky at the poles. Even where you might least expect it, you can still find yourself losing control on some slippery ice, so take care out there.

Back to you, Poppy.

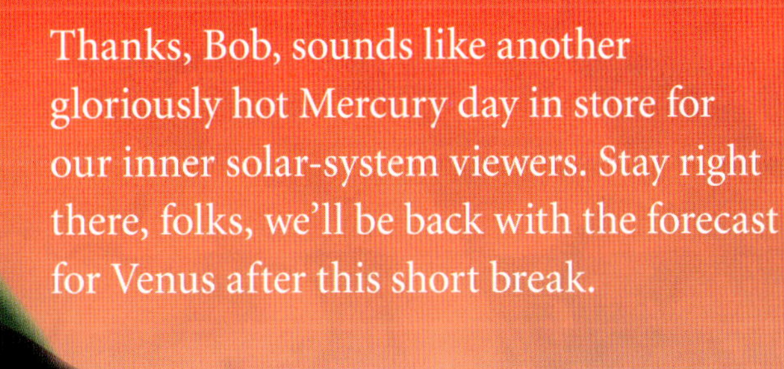

Thanks, Bob, sounds like another gloriously hot Mercury day in store for our inner solar-system viewers. Stay right there, folks, we'll be back with the forecast for Venus after this short break.

Sulfuric Acid **Showers**

You're back with tonight's edition of the Interplanetary Weather Bulletin. I'm Poppy Mono-Squint, and it's now time for Jim Slicky to update us on what you can expect in the vicinity of Venus over the next 24 hours.

INTERPLANETARY WEATHER BULLETIN

VENUS LIVE!

Poppy, it's a little after dawn here on Venus, the queen of the morning sky. As we rotate backwards, unlike all the other planets that rotate forwards, it was a lovely sunrise in the west. As you mentioned earlier, it's been about 480 °C here and we're not expecting much change over the next Venusian day – it takes a little over 116 Earth days from sunrise to sunrise here, so what you've been wearing over the last 24 hours will pretty much do you for the next 2 700 hours. It's hot enough to melt lead here, and that's not an exaggeration!

It's shaping up to be another cloudy and overcast day, which is much as we expected because that's the way it always is on Venus.

The thick carbon dioxide atmosphere will let the Sun's rays through to heat up the rocks on our surface, but then trap that heat, continuing to cause a "greenhouse" effect in all areas of the planet. It's a bit like winding all your windows up, then parking your car in a sunny spot for four billion years! There will be scattered showers of sulfuric acid from time to time, so acid-resistant gumboots might be the order of the day for those working outdoors. There's also a chance of thunder and lightning as clouds of sulfur dioxide acid jostle up against each other.

Slight winds are anticipated in equatorial areas, so if you're taking an umbrella, be careful. The wind might only move at two to three kilometres an hour, but because our atmospheric pressure is about 90 times higher than on Earth, they'll knock you over as if they were whistling past at 270 kilometres per hour. For those folks living in polar regions, you might want to consider staying indoors, as those winds will be rising to about 100 to 200 kilometres per hour. If you multiply that by a factor of 90, you'll see you'll need some super-heavy shoes to stay upright in those gusts!

That's Jim Slicky, reporting live from the hazy yellow surface of Venus, about 108 million kilometres from the Sun. That means the UV rays there will be about 1.3 times stronger than Earth, so make sure you keep some SPF 40 sunscreen on hand. Next up, we'll be taking a look at what the day holds for those of you on the third planet in the solar system, Earth.

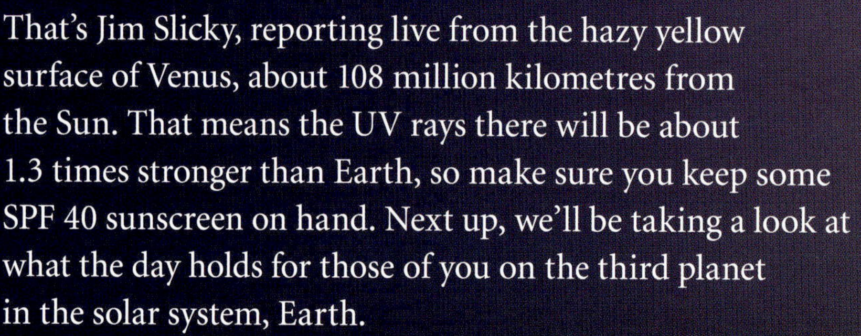

INTERPLANETARY WEATHER BULLETIN

WE'LL BE RIGHT BACK!

ULTRAVIOLET (UV) RAYS

Different wavelengths of light have different colours. Humans can see a spectrum of light from red, orange, yellow, green, blue, indigo and violet wavelengths. Ultraviolet rays are light that has a wavelength beyond violet light. This light, which is invisible to humans, causes sunburn.

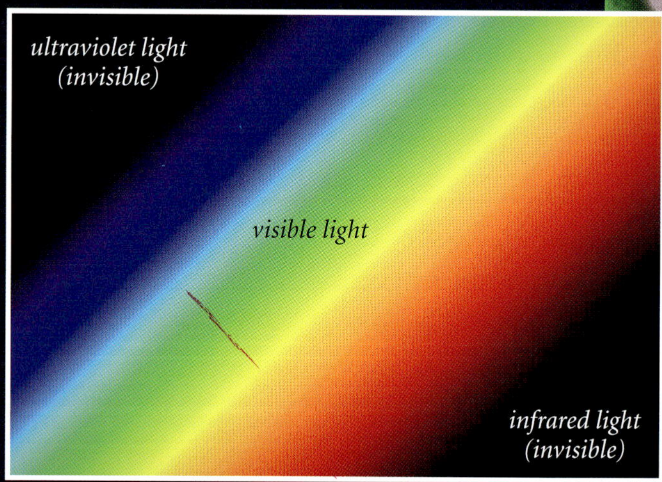

4 Earth

A Grim **Globe**

Thanks for staying with us, folks. I'm Poppy Mono-Squint, and this bulletin is coming to you from the Orbital Broadcasting Corporation's studio just beyond the asteroid belt between Mars and Jupiter. Now, let's cross to Jemima Dimple, who's waiting to join us from Earth. Jemima, can you hear me?

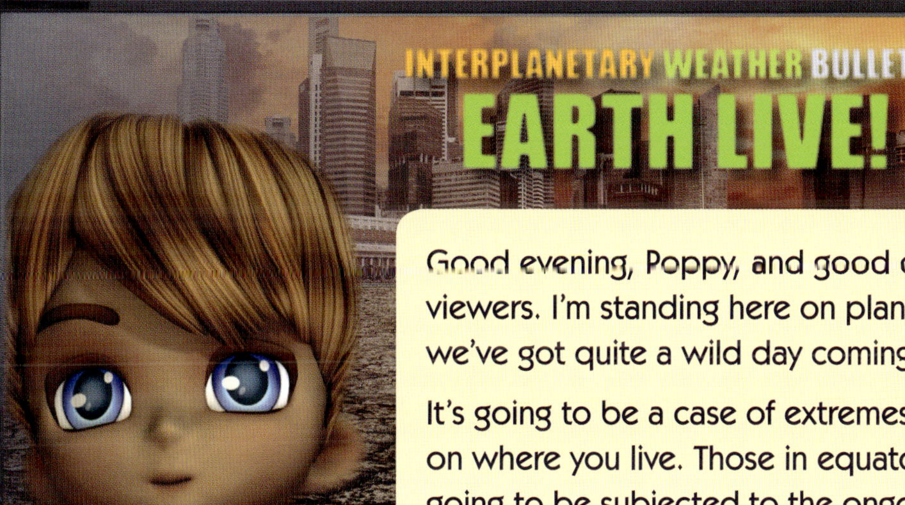

Good evening, Poppy, and good evening viewers. I'm standing here on planet Earth, and we've got quite a wild day coming up, I'm afraid.

It's going to be a case of extremes, depending on where you live. Those in equatorial areas are going to be subjected to the ongoing pattern of nasty heatwaves that Earth has been experiencing since global warming in the twenty-first century raised our temperatures far above the 4 °C average, as predicted by weather experts. Many areas in Africa, the Middle East and Asia will have another hot day in the 50 °C range, and there's little chance of rain.

Since the Greenland and Antarctic ice shelves melted, sea levels have risen to 6 metres above where they were in 2012, and that's bad news for anyone living on or near the coast. Tomorrow, because of the warmer sea temperatures, we're expecting more hurricanes to sweep over North America and Europe. We've gone from about three or four a year to about three or four a month now. Floods and storms are expected to continue in the planet's northernmost and southernmost areas, and the build-up of heavy, slightly acidic cloud cover due to industrial pollution will continue pretty much everywhere. As a consequence of the depletion of the ozone layer, if you're thinking of heading outside tomorrow, don't forget there are extreme UV alerts in place for all regions.

If you've got any of that Venusian SPF 40 sunscreen, it probably won't hurt to slap some on. We don't have quite the same conditions as Venus yet, but, due to the ongoing global warming resulting from the build-up of greenhouse gases here, some are saying it won't be too long before conditions really are pretty similar. Back to you, Poppy.

INTERPLANETARY WEATHER BULLETIN

STUDIO REACTION!

Thanks, Jemima, with that dire weather, it sounds like anywhere but Earth will be the place to be tomorrow. Stay tuned, because we'll be back with the latest Martian forecast, right after this break.

5 Mars

Dry and **Dusty**

You're watching the Interplanetary Weather Bulletin, and if you've been waiting for the weather on Mars, we're crossing right now to Lianne Smithers, who'll give us the latest update.

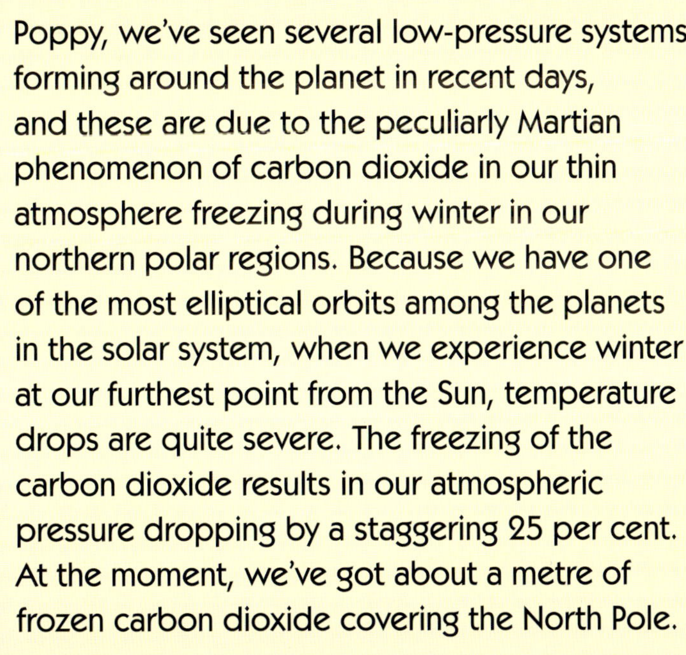

Poppy, we've seen several low-pressure systems forming around the planet in recent days, and these are due to the peculiarly Martian phenomenon of carbon dioxide in our thin atmosphere freezing during winter in our northern polar regions. Because we have one of the most elliptical orbits among the planets in the solar system, when we experience winter at our furthest point from the Sun, temperature drops are quite severe. The freezing of the carbon dioxide results in our atmospheric pressure dropping by a staggering 25 per cent. At the moment, we've got about a metre of frozen carbon dioxide covering the North Pole.

Generally, we're looking forward to a dry, clear and cold day on Mars tomorrow, with temperatures at the equator rising to a lovely 20 °C from their overnight lows of –90 °C. The northern polar regions, however, can look forward to another day of temperatures hovering around –140 °C, so you'll be needing the electric blanket and a hot water bottle if you're up there tonight.

Those variations in temperature at the equator mean a number of warm and cold fronts are mixing and, as a result, we've had reports of several dust storms sweeping across large areas of the planet. We're warning people to stay indoors if a dust storm approaches, as only the tiniest of particles can remain afloat in this thin atmosphere, and it's these particles that can pass through normal spacesuit filters and cause respiratory problems if they're inhaled.

PLANETARY NAMES

Apart from Earth, all the planets in the solar system are named after Roman gods:

Mercury	A messenger god
Venus	The god of romance
Mars	The god of war
Jupiter	The leader of the gods
Saturn	The god of agriculture
Uranus	The sky god
Neptune	The sea god
Pluto	The god of the underworld

a Martian dust devil

The severe and dusty weather conditions mean there's a chance of the occasional dust devil on Mars. For viewers from other planets, these are like towering tornados of dust that can reach several kilometres in height. We'll be posting dust-devil warnings on our website, so keep checking for updates over the next 24 hours and 39.5 minutes, which is our equivalent of a day.

Otherwise, there'll be plenty of beautiful light-brown sky to be seen over the planet, and we'll be experiencing lots of sunshine at about 40 per cent of the strength of that seen on Earth, so make the most of it, folks.

Lianne, thanks for that, and fingers crossed that no dust devils weave their way towards you. With water so short on Mars, it can be most irritating trying to wash those microscopic dust particles out of your hair. Stay tuned for Jupiter's weather, right after this short break.

Gigantic **Jupiter**

Hello again, I'm Poppy Mono-Squint, bringing you the latest weather updates from around the solar system. I'm speaking with Philip Jones, our man on the spot on Jupiter. Now, Philip, you've had a hurricane raging within your atmosphere for more than five hundred years. Any sign of those ferocious winds letting up?

Poppy, the gigantic hurricane we know as Jupiter's Great Red Spot has been raging for centuries now, sometimes growing to as large as 40 000 kilometres in diameter. The cloudy gales of ammonia blowing at around 360 kilometres per hour show no sign of abating, and the Great Red Spot is probably an area best avoided if you can help it.

Tomorrow is going to be pretty much the same as today, with the usual clouds of ammonia crystals swirling around the planet, carrying phosphorus and sulfur with them. The phosphorus and sulfur change colour when they're exposed to the sunlight, so folks on neighbouring planets see these as yellow, brown or white bands.

Because the thick atmosphere is so turbulent and stormy, we're expecting several towering thunderclouds to form. These warm, humid clouds typically rise about 50 kilometres above all the others. Beneath these clouds, we're forecasting quite a lot of lightning, which we're warning people to watch out for. Back on Earth, a bolt of lightning might have an electrical current of 30 000 amps, but everything's gigantic here, not just the planet, and a typical lightning bolt is about a thousand times more powerful.

Being a gas giant, with no actual surface, Jupiter's weather will consist mostly of huge, violent whirlpools of liquid gas, interspersed with periods of frozen gases falling from the murky skies and warmer gases from the planet's interior, spurting up into the atmosphere. And Poppy, as our magnetic field is about 14 times as strong as Earth's, we'll also be seeing some spectacular aurora skies around the polar regions, too, when that burst of solar wind you mentioned at the start of the program finally reaches us. All in all, we're in for a pretty rough 10-hour day here on the solar system's biggest planet, but that's par for the course here on Jupiter.

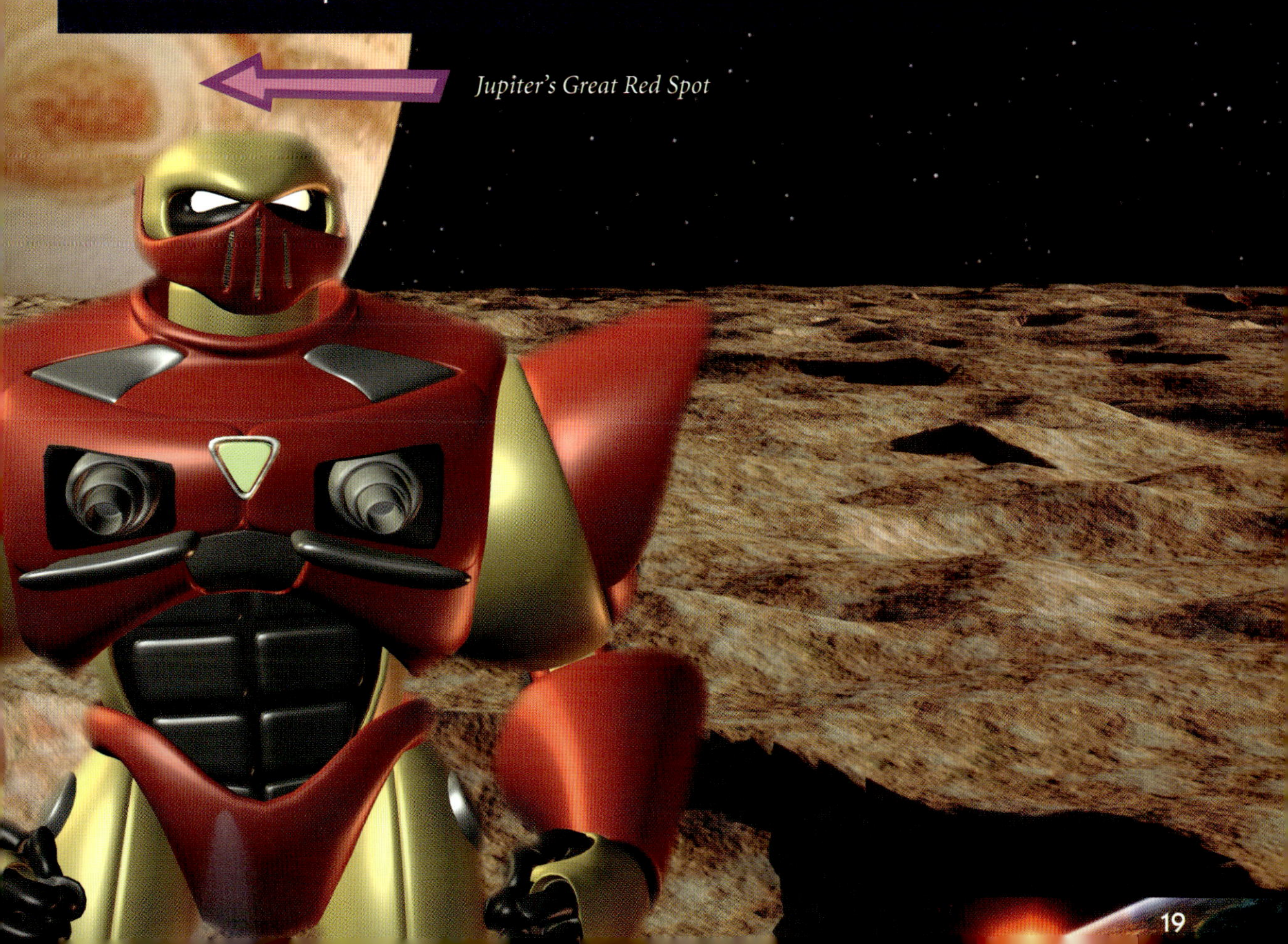

Jupiter's Great Red Spot

Thanks for that, Philip – you're back with Poppy now. With 500-year-old hurricanes raging across the atmosphere, Jupiter's weather makes the rest of us grateful that all we get are freezing clouds, scorching temperatures and planetary dust storms.

It's time for a short break, and then we'll be checking out what's happening beneath the rings of Saturn.

INTERPLANETARY WEATHER BULLETIN

WE'LL BE RIGHT BACK!

TERRESTRIAL OR GAS GIANT?

Be careful where you tread!

The inner four planets of the solar system (Mercury, Venus, Earth and Mars), along with the dwarf planet, Pluto, are known as terrestrial planets. They are solid, with a metallic core.

The outer planets (Jupiter, Saturn, Uranus and Neptune) are gas giants. They consist of swirling gases. The only solid material inside them is frozen or highly compressed gas. Curiously, all the gas giants have a number of rocky, terrestrial moons.

Regal Rings

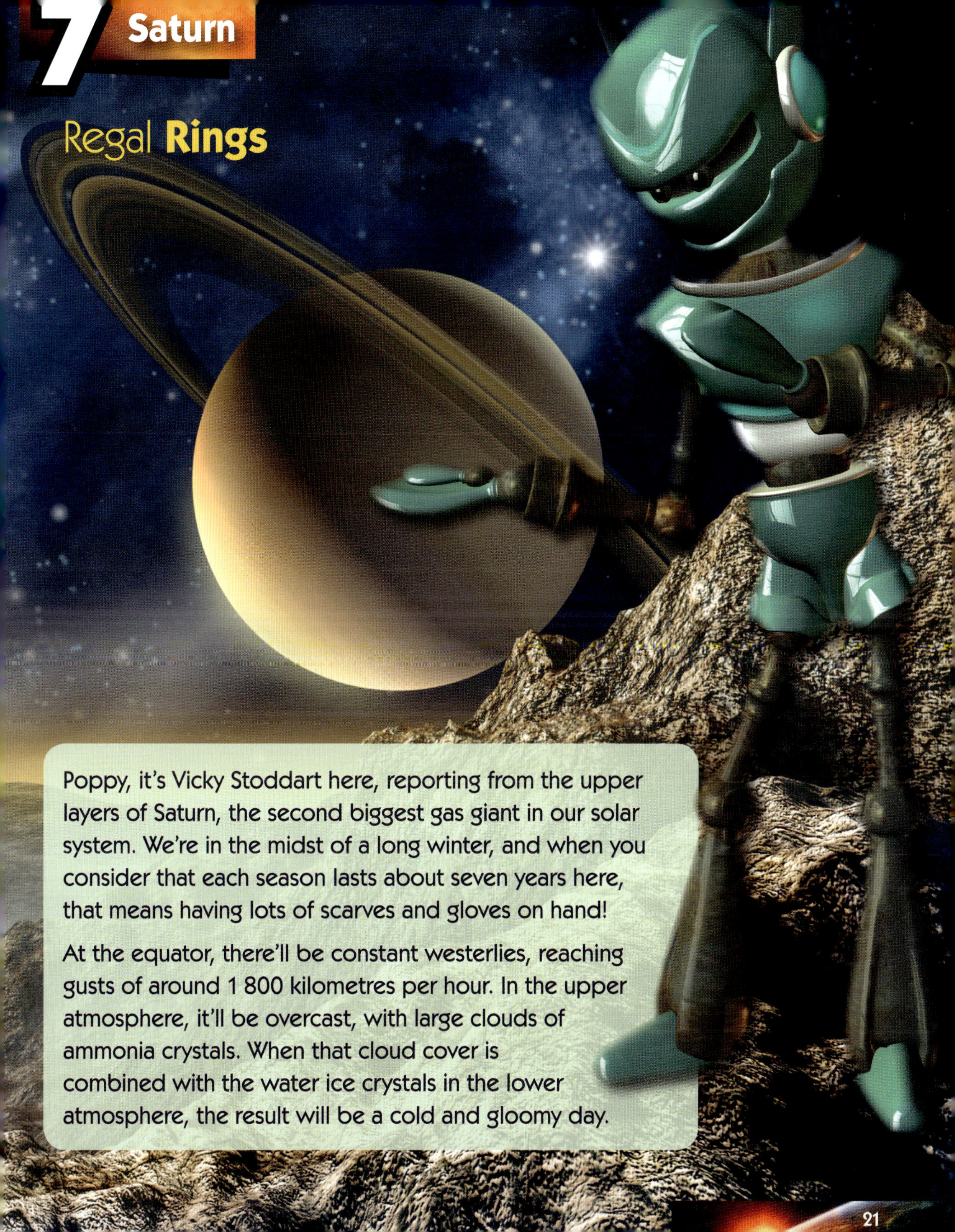

Poppy, it's Vicky Stoddart here, reporting from the upper layers of Saturn, the second biggest gas giant in our solar system. We're in the midst of a long winter, and when you consider that each season lasts about seven years here, that means having lots of scarves and gloves on hand!

At the equator, there'll be constant westerlies, reaching gusts of around 1 800 kilometres per hour. In the upper atmosphere, it'll be overcast, with large clouds of ammonia crystals. When that cloud cover is combined with the water ice crystals in the lower atmosphere, the result will be a cold and gloomy day.

Hot gases erupting from the centre of Saturn are forming a large anticyclone, similar to the Great Red Spot described by Philip in his Jupiter report. Our Great White Spot, as we like to call it, reappears every ten or so Earth years, but we're expecting it to only last a matter of months, so there'll be some relief shortly for those experiencing the high winds and frozen ammonia storms.

We have reports of powerful lightning bolts all over the planet. These can be even more spectacular than those on our neighbour, Jupiter, and we're seeing several thunderstorms, ranging in size from 5 000 to 10 000 kilometres in diameter.

There are a couple of stratospheric beacons causing concern at the moment, so watch out for those if you're planning a daytrip through Saturn's stratosphere. These are churning plumes of hot, supercharged ammonia, ammonium and hydrogen sulfide that rise about 300 kilometres above the surface clouds, so you can expect some severe turbulence in those regions. Keep your seatbelts on! Back to you, Poppy.

Thanks, Vicky, I'm sure you're looking forward to the Saturn spring when it finally arrives – but not as much as the folks on Uranus. They're just heading into autumn, and their seasons last for about 21 years. That means a long 42-year wait for spring to arrive. Luckily, you'll only have to wait for a minute or two for us to come back – right after these advertisements.

Cold and **Cloudy**

Next, we're crossing to Derek Gustafson, who's waiting about three billion kilometres away from the Sun, on Uranus. At that distance, our friendly yellow dwarf looks about a twentieth of the size it does on Earth. How are things shaping up weather-wise out there, Derek?

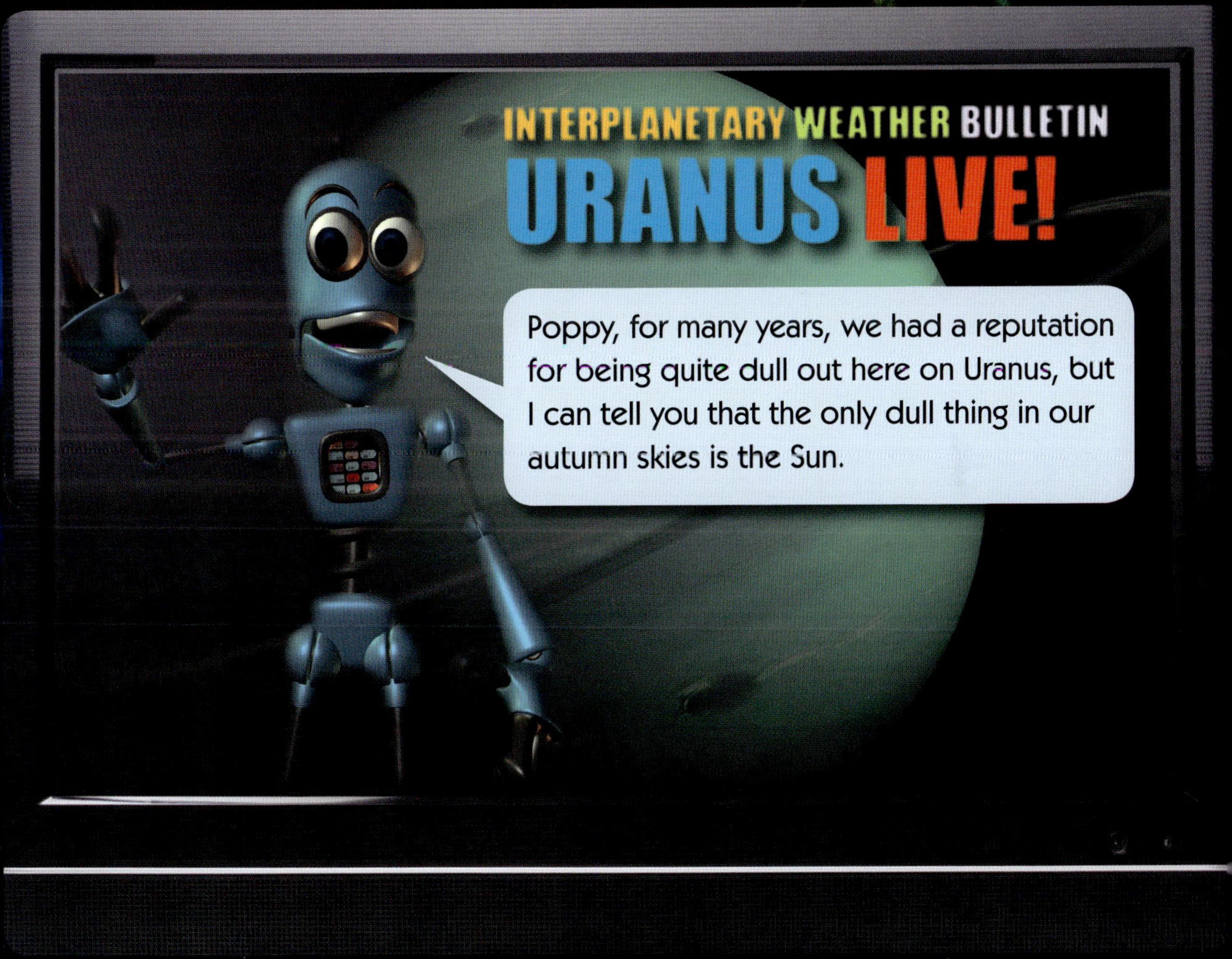

INTERPLANETARY WEATHER BULLETIN

URANUS LIVE!

Poppy, for many years, we had a reputation for being quite dull out here on Uranus, but I can tell you that the only dull thing in our autumn skies is the Sun.

As summer drew to a close here on Uranus, we saw a number of huge methane storm clouds brewing up through the blue–green haze that coats most of our planet. The winds in these storm systems are picking up speed to around 420 kilometres per hour. Over summer, we only had around 30 clouds visible in the sky – so even though the clouds were about 29 000 kilometres long, we had plenty of fine periods in between, because most of them only lasted for a month or so. Of course, I use the term "fine" in relative terms. It's still averaging around a chilly –180 °C because, as you said, Poppy, when you're this far out there's not much danger of getting sunburnt. The amount of sunlight we get here is about one-four-hundredth of what Earth receives.

As autumn progresses, we can expect the slushy water, ammonia and methane that covers the surface of Uranus to start freezing. Although we're not the furthest planet from the Sun in the solar system, ever since Pluto was demoted to a dwarf planet we have the dubious honour of being the coldest, due to the fact that we don't have much warmth coming from our core. Luckily, we've got another 21 years to get ready for the worst that winter can throw at us, and we'll need it, with temperatures plummeting to as low as –224 °C and wind speeds accelerating as high as 900 kilometres per hour.

Freezing Forecast

Nancy, I understand you're experiencing some of the most violent weather in the solar system there on Neptune. Tell us what's happening over there.

That's right, Poppy, we've been seeing winds on Neptune clocking around 2 100 kilometres per hour, which is almost four times as fast as those recorded on Jupiter. These are westerlies, as most of our strong winds blow in the opposite direction to our rotation, and they're mostly hydrogen, helium and methane, with a scattering of frozen ammonium thrown in for good measure. Luckily, the Great Dark Spot, which was a huge anticyclone covering about 86 million square kilometres, has blown itself out, but several smaller storms are raging across our surface right now, and the fear is that they'll join up and deliver us a superstorm.

We're so far out that we get around 40 per cent less sunlight than our friends on neighbouring Uranus, but we do have much higher temperatures in our planetary core, and it's these that form the giant gas vortexes that eventually manifest themselves as turbulent storms.

It doesn't help that our polar regions rotate faster than our equatorial regions, as this causes some pretty strong wind shear patterns across the middle of our planet.

I think it's safe to say that we can expect continued gusty winds, overcast skies and freezing temperatures for at least the next 40 years, which is when the seasons will start to change – probably for the worse. Over to Pluto, and our provincial reporter, Chuck McCluskey!

Thanks, Nancy. Poppy, Pluto's weather can be pretty much summed up in one word: cold. In fact, it's so cold here that as we move even further away from the Sun, our entire atmosphere of nitrogen, methane and carbon dioxide just freezes and falls as snow.
At our furthest orbit, we'll be about 7.2 billion kilometres from the Sun, so far, in fact, that it'll just look like another star among all the others in our night sky.

Right now, as I look at the temperature gauge, it's plumbing depths of around –235 °C, which is not far away from the absolute minimum temperature possible anywhere in the universe, –273 °C. This means we'll need to look out for widespread areas of nitrogen frost forming overnight. Back to you, Poppy.

Thanks, Chuck. And that's our regional weather wrap-up for the solar system tonight. No matter where you are, no matter what your weather holds in store, and no matter how long your day is, we hope you have a great one.
I'm Poppy Mono-Squint, and you've been watching the Interplanetary Weather Bulletin, broadcast throughout the solar system by the Orbital Broadcasting Corporation. Goodnight!

10 Global Warming

A Planetary **Climate Challenge**

For some years, people have been aware that Earth's climate is changing, as evidenced by the average increases in temperature over time. Climate science research indicates that the activities of humans are contributing to the changes being observed. By investigating planets where extreme climate changes have already taken place, astronomers and other space scientists can construct a picture of what might happen on Earth if the planet continues to grow warmer.

Scientific data indicates that Earth's temperatures have risen with the increase of greenhouse gases, such as carbon dioxide and methane, in the atmosphere. Climate scientists have shown that a number of other planets in the solar system with quantities of carbon dioxide and methane in their atmosphere have also experienced climate change. Mars may once have had a denser atmosphere, with significant amounts of liquid water, and Venus has been experiencing global warming through the effects of greenhouse gases for millions of years. By studying the effects of greenhouse gases on other planets, climate scientists can draw conclusions about the future of Earth.

measuring climate change in the Arctic

EVIDENCE OF CLIMATE CHANGE

Scientists use a range of methods to determine historical changes in climate over periods of time. Human records only exist for perhaps the most recent thousand years, but many other natural observations help to chart changes over much longer periods. Pollen samples, patterns of vegetation, air bubbles trapped in Antarctic ice sheets, geological evidence of ancient sea levels, the shape of landscapes around glaciers and even tree rings can be used to determine increases or decreases in global temperatures. Even the distribution of human archaeological sites, which change according to climate and population, can give clues about historical weather patterns.

Water is another indicator of climate, both for hypothesising about past events and for predicting the future. The geology of Venus indicates that it once had oceans, but after millions of years of greenhouse gases warming that planet, its oceans evaporated and disappeared. While this outcome may be unlikely on Earth, with increasingly warm temperatures it is possible that the vast amounts of ice in Antarctica and Greenland could melt. If the amount of liquid water on Earth increases sufficiently, sea levels could rise by as much as six metres. As a result, many low-lying areas, such as South-East Asia, the islands of the Pacific and huge areas of continental coastline could end up underwater.

Venus once had oceans.

Glacial ice melts and falls into the ocean.

WATER, WATER EVERYWHERE (BUT NOT A DROP TO DRINK)

Rising temperatures on Earth may also cause glaciers to eventually disappear, and many of the world's major rivers may dry up. In areas such as India, where glaciers in the Himalayas are the source of water for the Ganges River, this could lead to devastating consequences for the 500 million people who rely on that water for drinking and irrigation.

People use water from the Ganges River for drinking, bathing, sanitation and irrigation.

By recording the effects of temperature variations on different planets, scientists can predict likely outcomes for Earth. For example, on Mars, extreme temperature variations result in severe dust storms; on Jupiter and Saturn, differences in temperature between hot internal gases and colder surface gases cause gigantic hurricanes. As with other planets, Earth's storms and other violent weather events are driven by variations in temperature in the ocean. If Earth's oceans continue to get warmer, there may be an increase in the number and severity of hurricanes and other storm systems, while on land there may be an increase in the frequency and severity of heatwaves.

a severe Martian dust storm forms

a Mars Lander searches for evidence of life

The lack of evidence of life on other planets in the solar system demonstrates the narrow range of temperatures and climatic conditions required for living things to exist. While temperature variations on Earth are tiny compared to other planets, humans experience many health conditions related to relatively small changes in climate, ranging from heat-related heart and respiratory issues through to diseases found in warmer, tropical areas, such as malaria and other insect-borne illnesses. For this reason, health workers have concerns about the spread of climate-related illnesses in a warmer global environment.

By studying the extreme climatic conditions of Earth's neighbouring planets, scientists hope to better understand the ways that extreme global-warming conditions impact on weather, and how this weather can in turn impact on the conditions that are vital for life to exist. Earth has exactly the right combination of energy, chemicals and physical environment to allow life to flourish, and humans need to do their utmost to ensure that they do not upset this apparently unique and delicate balance.

Index

Glossary

atmosphere The mass of air, made up of gas, surrounding Earth or other celestial bodies

climate change Changes in Earth's climate over a long period of time, due to natural factors or human activity

dust devil A strong whirlwind, similar to a tornado, that forms in response to a surface heating up in dry, hot weather

dwarf star A star, such as the Sun, with low mass, small size and below-average luminosity

equator The imaginary circle around Earth's surface, dividing Earth into the Northern Hemisphere and the Southern Hemisphere

fluctuation To vary irregularly, or to rise and fall in waves

orb A celestial body, such as the Sun or a moon

supergiant A large, bright star, with a luminosity thousands of times greater than that of the Sun

turbulent Wild, disturbed or chaotic

vortex A spiral motion of fluid within a certain area, which sucks everything near it towards its centre